MADRONA

I like the
WIND

written by Sarah Nelson • illustrated by Rachel Oldfield

Barefoot Books
step inside a story

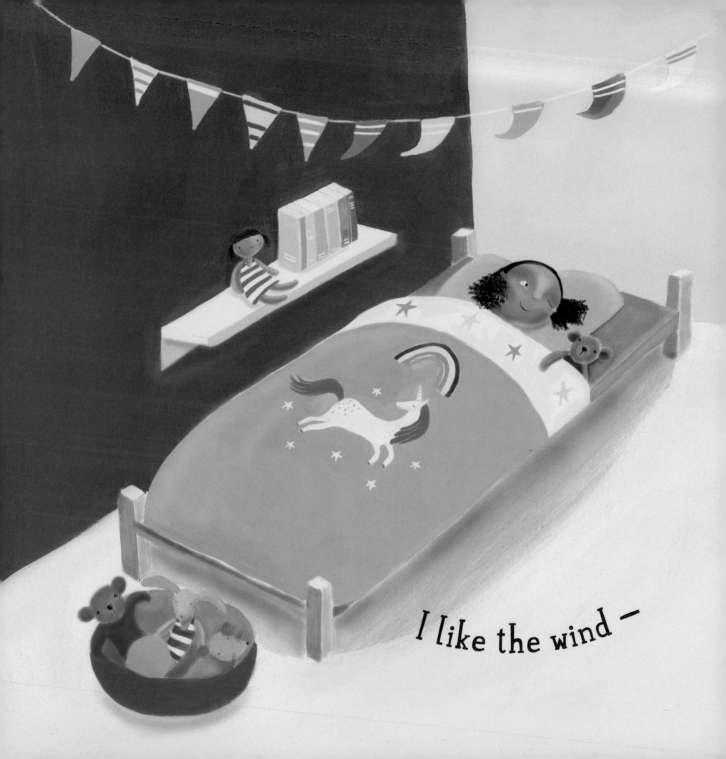

I like the wind —

whistling "wake up" in my ears.
Swee-swoo! "Come play out here!"

Wispy whispers on my cheeks.
This is how the wind speaks.

I like the wind –
I throw on shoes and grab my kite,

then down the stairs and off in flight.

I like racing wind on two fast feet,
a swirl of leaves along the street.

Wind whirls and whips and hums and flips.

Clouds go by like towering ships.

I like the sudden, quiet hushes . . .
splatters of rain in gusting rushes.

Windy whooshes! Howling roars!

Shivering windows and rattling doors!

Bowing branches bending low,
swinging apples to and fro.

I like it when the wild wind calms
and opens up its mouth and yawns.

It slowly blows the sun away

and pulls the dark across the day.

Shhhh . . .

I like the wind.

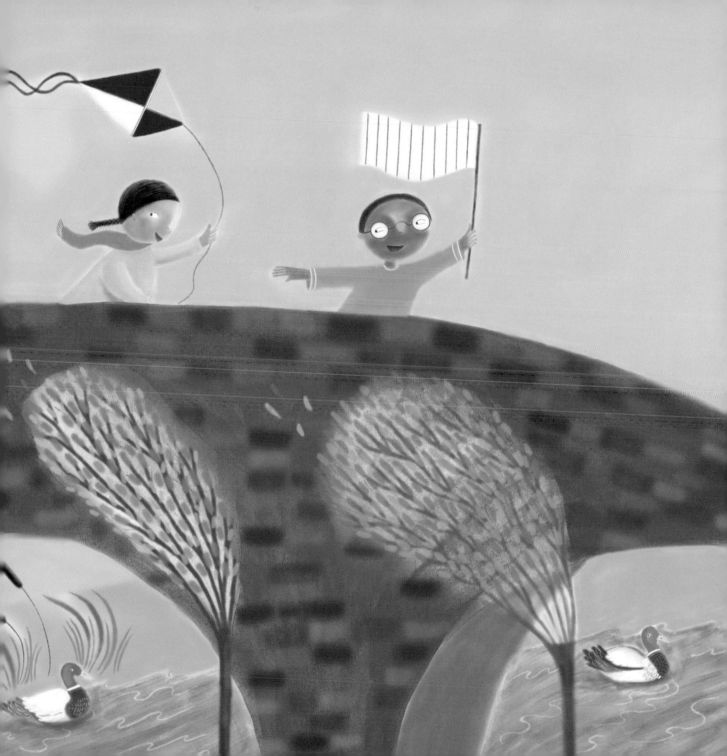

Questions for a Windy Day

Why does wind blow?

Our Earth is surrounded by layers of air. The layer of air closest to us is where weather happens. This air is almost always on the move. The sun warms up some parts of the Earth more than others. When air gets warm, it rises up and makes a space. Then cooler air rushes in to fill that space. That's wind!

Why is it windy at the beach?

Have you ever lost your sun hat on a windy beach? Strong winds often blow in from the ocean (or a large lake) because land warms up faster than water on a sunny day. As warm air rises from a hot, sunny beach, it leaves a space for cooler ocean air to rush in. After the sun sets, the wind may reverse as the land cools more quickly than the water.

What is wind power?

Windy weather can make electricity with the help of wind turbines. Turbines are tall structures with large blades. When wind blows, it spins these blades, and the turbines change the energy of the wind into electric energy. Wind is a source of energy that doesn't pollute and can never be used up.

How does wind help us?

In addition to making electricity, the wind gives us many other gifts. It blows rain clouds around the planet, delivering fresh water to trees, food crops, thirsty animals and us. Wind scatters pollen and seeds so that plants can grow. Wind flies flags, sails boats and helps propel migrating birds and even planes. Thank you, wind!

Enjoy more weather fun with *I Like the Snow*, *I Like the Rain* and *I Like the Sun*.

In memory of my mom, who thought a windy day was most exciting — S. N.

For my niece and nephew Fern and Merry, and in loving memory of Arthur — R. O.

Barefoot Books
2067 Massachusetts Ave
Cambridge, MA 02140

Barefoot Books
29/30 Fitzroy Square
London, W1T 6LQ

Text copyright © 2021 by Sarah Nelson
Illustrations copyright © 2021 by Rachel Oldfield
The moral rights of Sarah Nelson and Rachel Oldfield have been asserted

First published in United States of America by Barefoot Books, Inc
and in Great Britain by Barefoot Books, Ltd in 2021. All rights reserved

Graphic design by Elizabeth Kaleko, Barefoot Books
Edited and art directed by Kate DePalma, Barefoot Books
Reproduction by Bright Arts, Hong Kong

Printed in China on 100% acid-free paper
This book was typeset in Century Gothic, Cut-Out,
Dear St. Nick and Mr Lucky
The illustrations were prepared in acrylics

Hardback ISBN 978-1-64686-094-4 • E-book ISBN 978-1-64686-020-3

British Cataloguing-in-Publication Data:
a catalogue record for this book is available from the British Library

Library of Congress Cataloging-in-Publication Data
is available under LCCN 2020009336

1 3 5 7 9 8 6 4 2

Barefoot Books
Step inside a story

At Barefoot Books, we celebrate art and story that opens the hearts and minds of children from all walks of life, focusing on themes that encourage independence of spirit, enthusiasm for learning and respect for the world's diversity. The welfare of our children is dependent on the welfare of the planet, so we source paper from sustainably managed forests and constantly strive to reduce our environmental impact. Playful, beautiful and created to last a lifetime, our products combine the best of the present with the best of the past to educate our children as the caretakers of tomorrow.

www.barefootbooks.com

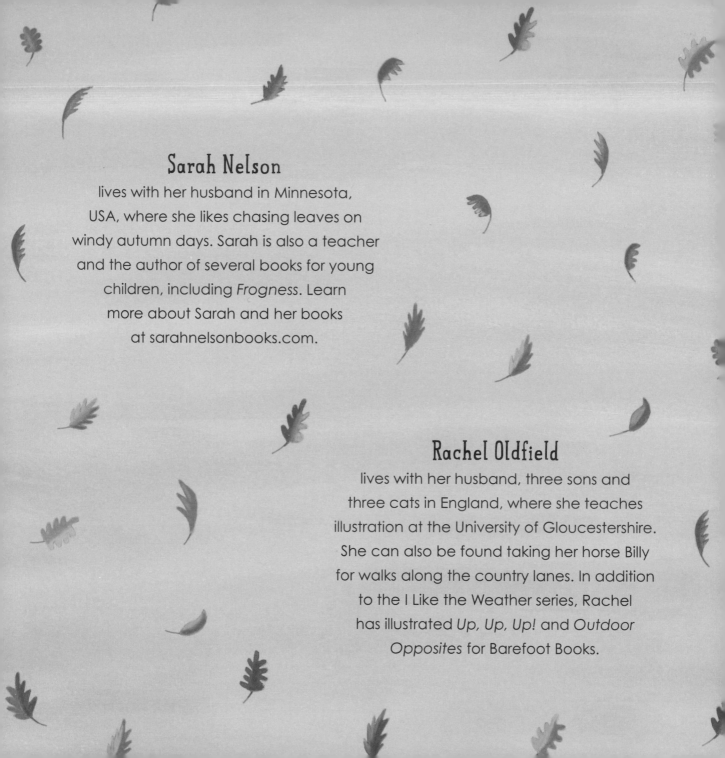

Sarah Nelson

lives with her husband in Minnesota,
USA, where she likes chasing leaves on
windy autumn days. Sarah is also a teacher
and the author of several books for young
children, including *Frogness*. Learn
more about Sarah and her books
at sarahnelsonbooks.com.

Rachel Oldfield

lives with her husband, three sons and
three cats in England, where she teaches
illustration at the University of Gloucestershire.
She can also be found taking her horse Billy
for walks along the country lanes. In addition
to the I Like the Weather series, Rachel
has illustrated *Up, Up, Up!* and *Outdoor
Opposites* for Barefoot Books.